Good Girl Gone Bad

written by
Vanessa Daze

authorHOUSE®

AuthorHouse™
1663 Liberty Drive
Bloomington, IN 47403
www.authorhouse.com
Phone: 1-800-839-8640

First published by AuthorHouse 01/05/2009

ISBN: 978-1-4490-6575-1 (e)
ISBN: 978-1-4490-6574-4 (sc)

Printed in the United States of America
Bloomington, Indiana

This book is printed on acid-free paper.

"to everyone out there who feel like they have to become somebody else just to fit in."

Introduction

Although Good Girls Gone Bad is about the life of a teenager, the book is designed for any age group. It encompasses many themes and notions that we can all relate to. What inspired me to write this book were all of the experiences such as popularity issues, bullies and peer-pressures that I made throughout my whole life especially in school. I myself as the writer have learned a lot from the story that is being told in the book and I really hope that each and every one of you who actually reads this book can also learn a lot from it and can also relate to it in a particular way because there is a true story of ardent love, family, friendship, and sorrow behind it.

Going to a new city and starting a new life can be very challenging for a teenage girl. You have to make new friends, start everything over. Well, did it really matter for me? Nobody ever paid attention to me in Kentucky. No one besides my parents and the blind lady next door has ever told me "Victoria, you're a beautiful girl." At school, I was always known for the math geek, the unimportant girl. I was best known for the girl who puked in ninth grade in front of the whole school. What a shame, that day I swore I would never go back to school. I was raised in a poor family, with nothing but a family farm. Who would pay attention to a girl like me? Where I'm from to be noticed, you had to be the richest or the hottest girl at school. Kentucky is my hometown, I was born and raised there; and I hated it there, I hated my grandpa's farm, my school, my peers, I hated everyone. I used to say that I would do anything to be popular, I would just do anything for a guy to tell me "hey, Victoria would you like to be my date for the homecoming dance? " Or "hey Victoria, this dress looks great on you". I would do just about anything for the popular girls to tell me" Hey, Vickie want to hang out at the mall? "My only friends were my parents. God I hated my life, I just wanted to leave, go far away, to another country where I would meet new people and be different. Well, sadly, I guess my wish came true, in a different way. When my father died, he left me and my mother fifty million dollars. If you're wondering how such a poor family can have fifty million dollars, well I think you have the answer, lottery of course.

My mother's name was Lisa. She was the sweetest woman I've never met and she loved me more than anything in the world. After my father's death, she wanted to start a new life and get rid of the unbearable memories. I guess even her was tired of the boring old small town life. Everyday was the same; working on the farm, hoping to get some milk from Tina, our cow. We decided to move to Los Angeles. I always wanted to go leave there. I heard, that was just a beautiful place and maybe who knows I could be the next prom queen there. My mother wanted to surprise me, I've never leaved in a house before, and the farm was my home. When I arrived to Los Angeles, everything looked so different; in my head I was thinking that's my only chance to have my dream come true, to be noticed, to be popular.

I remember the look at my mother's face when she saw how happy I was admiring the new city. It's like watching a little girl taking her first baby steps or her first words. " I'm glad you like it honey", she said with a beautiful smile.

I was so excited to see my new house; again I've never been to a real house before. One of the biggest moments of my life was when I got inside my house; that was totally not what I was expecting. My crib was the most beautiful crib I had ever seen in my life, everything looked so shiny, I felt like I was in a beautiful dream and I didn't want to wake up from it. I kept saying "wow! Mom this is our home". All I could do was hugging my mom, telling her how much I love her for this house, how much it means to me to finally live like a person and not a cow.

My mom who has never been in a house herself was as happy as I was; I remember her saying with tears of happiness "do you know how long I've been waiting to give you this honey"? That was truly one of the best moments me and my mom shared, unfortunately my dad didn't get to see this gorgeous house. He would have loved it as much as we did.

So here I was, standing in my room and admiring everything, the first time that I had my own room and a bed. I was an only child. I always referred to the animals from my old farm as siblings since I grew up with them and they were my only friends besides my parents.

I didn't want to go to sleep the day I saw my house, I just wanted to walk around the house and touch everything. I just wanted to play with everything like a little child. But I remember my mom saying "honey, you have to go to bed now, you'll have time admire your house, remember tomorrow is your first day of school".

The word "school" made me sick. It's not that I didn't like school, I actually loved school and I was doing very well in it. I was a straight As student with the hope of becoming a lawyer, but honestly went I moved here, all I could think about was the kids, how my life would change. Would the kids from my school be the same as the previous one? Because if they were, I swear I would live the country or even kill myself.

My mom drove me to school on the first day of school; in a car, not a horse. That was the best feeling ever, finally to ride in a car and not walking twenty miles to go to the grocery store.

Standing in front of the school, my mom said "well this is it honey, have a nice first day of school".

As excited as I was to be in a new school, I was very nervous. I looked around and I saw the kids going psycho. Trust me, I know what that word means, I've seen kids at my old school in Kentucky do crazy things, but these ones looked so evil, I could just read EVIL in their face. I kept comparing my clothes to them, I kept watching the girls, the hot cheerleaders, the girls with the tight shirts, and me I was simply wearing a blue dress that I got for my eleventh birthday and some red shoes. All of a sudden, as I saw all of these kids so different than me, I felt like I was again in Kentucky, ready to be humiliated, I didn't want my mom to leave me. I hold her arm real tight and I told her "mom, these kids are so different, do you think they're going to make fun of me". And of course like any mother would say my mom answered" why would they? You'll be fine honey. Listen I know you're nervous and it's okay but trust me in less than a week all of these girls will be your friend. You promise, I said with a quaking voice. "Of course", answered my mom, "now go, I love you". My mom gave me a big kiss on my cheeks leaving her lipsticks all over, I was pretty embarrassed. I even remember one of the girls saying this is high school god damn it. It is true that my mom thought I was still a three year old child, she treated me like one. Literally I wasn't, I was seventeen years old and a senior in high school.

The first thing I saw when I walked in the school was a hot cheerleader making out with a guy. I starred at them as if I was getting kissing lessons. Then a girl came by me and said "what you're never seen a whore exchanging saliva before, well welcome to the real world". She introduced herself to me by shaking her hands with me, "I'm Tamara so are you new" she said. "Yes I just transfer here from a small town in Kentucky", I replied. As I kept watching the cheerleader making out with the guy who I supposed was her boyfriend, I asked Tamara who they were. "Let's just say someone that you'll wish you never talk to and the meanest and most popular bitch in this school", she answered. So does she have a name I asked? Gwen, she answered, her name is Gwen. Tamara was one of the people that I probably would not want as my friend because she looked like a nerd. She was wearing about the same clothes as me and I just wanted to talk to Gwen.

As I looked the other way, I saw Gwen and two other girls heading to us. All three of them were cheerleaders, all eyes were on them. At this moment I felt like I wanted to be one of them. "Oh look who we got here, an exchange student from Mars is that right." Gwen said. As soon as she said that, one of the girls kept laughing, she kept looking me up and down as if she wanted to tell me to get some real clothes. "It's not funny; just leave her alone, you don't even know her", Tamara said. "You're right I don't, and I never will, let's go girls", Gwen said. I never had anyone stand up for me like Tamara did, I felt like I owed her the world for actually stand up for me in such a situation. I kept thinking maybe Tamara is my one true friend, one that can stand up for you me. As Gwen walked by me I felt disappointed, insulted; I just couldn't believe Gwen said that to me, I felt like crying but I didn't. The day I left Kentucky, I promised myself that I would be strong, that was the whole point of starting a new life.

"Are you okay, Vickie, Tamara Said?"

"Yeah I guess"

"I'm so sorry"

"No, don't be, I get that a lot. It's not the first time someone has said that to me, trust me, I've been through worst times."

"I won't let anyone treat you like that again, Victoria."

"Thanks and thank you for standing up for me, that meant a lot to me. So, who where these girls anyways?"

"As you know, the one who insulted you was Gwen, and the two other ones are Alicia and Stacey."

Gwen, Alicia, Stacey, Chris and Sam sat down at a table at lunch. Gwen and Alicia were cheerleaders and Chris and Sam were played football at the High School. They all looked so happy, so beautiful. These are the kind of people I wanted as my friends; I thought they would give me popularity. I kept starring at them the whole time in their conversation.

Chris: Dude, you know who that was.

Gwen: I think I saw it all, probably one of the exchange student.

Sam: I heard that's the new geek who just transferred here from Kentucky.

Chris: And you know what else I heard.

Gwen: what?

Chris: Her father just died recently leaving them fifty millions dollars.

Gwen: She is one hell of a lucky girl. Welcome to the bitch club honey.

Alicia: You're not thinking about being friend with her are you?

Gwen: Of course not, sometimes you need to pretend you like people, just to get on their skin. See if we pretend to become friends with her, we'll make sure we get what she has.

Stacey: Her money, no she would not give us her money, forget it.

Gwen: Would you shut up. Honey, geeks can do anything for you when you pretend you love them. I will do to her the same thing that I did to the others, except this time my plan will actually work.

Sam: Whatever it is, as long as I'm making money, I'm down with it.

Gwen: That's why I love you Sam; really you are the smartest guy ever.

Chris: Hello, I'm in too.

Alicia: So, am I.

Gwen: So are you in this Stacey.

Stacey: Why should I. You've done this to me too. The same thing you want to do with whatever her name is you've done it to me.

Gwen: You know that's not true, she's a nerd and she needs help, you didn't. You were perfect.

Stacey: But, you never liked me as a friends, you wanted something from me.

Gwen: Getting me a bag.

Stacey: A bag of cocaine, I could have gotten arrested.

Gwen: Stacey, that happened three years ago, get over it. I know you want to do this, listen here's the deal, you don't have to do anything but watch our back and when we get her money, I'll give you one hundred thousand dollars, now that's a big step in paying your college tuition. So can we count you in?

Stacey: I guess.

Gwen: Well done.

At lunch, I sat with Tamara. I didn't want to seat with Tamara; well did I have any other choice? In my old school, I was one of the geeks who is always reading alone in lunch time. No one has ever told me to sit with them or to have lunch with them. When I wanted to eat, I would eat in the restroom so no one would tell me "All of these chips will make you fat". I've been called fat a couple of times. My mother thought I was the thinnest girl she's ever seen but I didn't think so.

Tamara seemed a very nice girl. I could tell she was a good and honest person since the first time we talked. While talking to Tamara, a guy appeared; that was Tamara's friend.

"Hey guys, you must be Victoria the new girl."

"Yes I am"

"I'm Matt, nice to meet you".

Matt kept talking the entire time. He did seem like a pretty nice guy, but I stopped paying attention to him when I saw this adorable guy sitting at Gwen's table. "Who is this guy" I asked. "His name is Sam, he is one of the biggest jerks that you'd wish you never knew", answered Tamara". "He dated all the girls at school", added Matt. I really didn't care what Tamara and Matt were saying about Sam, I thought he was really cute.

All of a sudden, while talking to Tamara and Sam I saw Gwen, Stacey and Alicia approaching to my table. If they had insulted me again, I swear I would stand up for myself for once in my life.

Gwen: Hey, um... Victoria is that right.

Victoria: Yeah

Gwen: I just want to apologize for the way we just treated you, that's really not the kind of people we are.

Tamara: (whispering) yeah right.

Victoria: Apology accepted.

Gwen: So would you like to sit with us.

Victoria: Really. Well I guess you're not as mean as I've been told.

When Gwen proposed me to seat with her, if felt like that was a dream come true. I didn't care about what she said to me. With no hesitation, I accepted their demand.

Tamara: Oh my god, she is totally in the wrong group.

Matt: What should we do? You think she'll be fine.

Tamara: You know Gwen, she just uses people, and she doesn't care about anybody.

Matt: Why would she use Victoria?

Tamara: Because her father just died a year ago leaving her and her mom fifty million dollars.

Matt: How do you know all these things?

Tamara: It was all over the newspaper.

Matt: Bet this money will really help Gwen and her mom to pay their drug's debt. Victoria is a nice girl; we can't let that happen to her.

Tamara: Let's wait and see what happens.

Sitting with Gwen and her friends was just a long period of interrogation. They wanted to know every little detail about me. The only quiet one was Stacey; at first I actually thought she was mute.

Alicia: So Tamara, why did you transfer here?

Victoria: Well my father just died a year ago and my mom wanted to come here and start a new life.

Gwen: Sorry about your father, so where are you from.

Victoria: Kentucky.

Chris: How do you like the new city?

Victoria: I love it, I just love it.

Alicia: How do you like the school?

Victoria: I love it, I just love it.

Gwen: That must be really sad to lose somebody you love, do you want to come over my house after school, and you know we can hang out, have fun.

Victoria: Umm. Sure... why not.

When Gwen offered me to hang out with her, I was thrilled. I didn't want to show her that I was waiting for this question so I simply answered sure... why not, but the happiness was burning inside of me. I felt like my dream has finally come true.

When the school bell rang, Gwen, Alicia, Stacey, Sam, Chris was waiting for me in Gwen's car.

Chris: You know if it wasn't because of that money, I would make that geek's life miserable.

Gwen: I know right.

Alicia: Remember what we did last year to that new kid from jersey.

Sam: That bitch just had to leave the school

Due to all the respect I had for my dear mother, I called her first to let her know that I was staying over Gwen's house. As I approached to Gwen and her friends I heard them talking. I couldn't exactly hear what they were saying but, I hoped they were they were just saying how excited they were to hang out with me.

Sam: She's coming.

Gwen: Let's all just pretend to be nice.

Gwen: Hey Victoria, where were you, we've been waiting for you for half an hour.

Victoria: I'm sorry I had to make a phone call to my mom to let her know that I will be coming home late.

Chris: Little girl got to ask her mommy her permission.

Gwen hit Sam on his stomach as is she was trying to tell him shut up, what the hell are you doing, be nice damn it. I laughed pretending it was funny, but really I felt uncomfortable.

Gwen: Victoria, this is Sam.

Victoria: Hello.

Sam: Hey

Gwen: And this is my boyfriend Chris.

Chris: Welcome to the no geek club.

Gwen: Shut up. I hope you don't take it personal Victoria; we just like to joke around.

Victoria: Sure.

Gwen: So are you ready.

Victoria: Yeah

Gwen: Bye

Chris: I love you.

Gwen: I love you too.

Chris and Sam left us. I really wanted Sam to come with us, he looked so adorable that I just wanted to grab him and kiss him. I just couldn't believe it, on my first day of school, I got to talk to the most popular kids at school. For once, I loved my life, I loved my new life so much that I totally forgot about my poor father.

We were all inside of the car while suddenly Gwen turned the music on. As soon as the Jay-z song popped on, everyone were singing, dancing and having fun except for me of course. Not that I wasn't having fun, I was happy to be there with them but at first I did feel a little uncomfortable being the only one who seriously knew nothing about Hip Hop and all the variety of music that a typical seventeen year old girl would fall for. When I was in Kentucky, I didn't have a TV or a radio at home, surprised but we couldn't afford one. Gwen was the loudest one in the car, she kept singing and dancing, I was even scared that we might have an accident. "Come on Victoria, sing, what kind of music are you into"? She asked. "Church, you know gospel" I answered.

They all laughed. I made a fool of myself by saying this, I felt stupid and I felt like I could have possibly ruined myself of being friends with Gwen. I couldn't think of anything else but church. Therefore it is true that the only songs I knew were from my church, I also have a few ones that I remember from preschool.

Alicia: gospel... Girl how old are you besides this is L.A. and you have to stop that geek thing.

Victoria: Pardon me.

Gwen: Come on Vicky don't take it personal, what Alicia meant what as our friend now, and you're going to be into the same thing things we're into, isn't that right Stacey.

Stacey: Yeah totally, you're one of us now.

Gwen: We're the hottest girls at the school and so will you, Vicky.

Victoria: So what are you saying?

Gwen: I'm saying that these clothes got to go. Come on in.

My first time at Gwen's house felt like I was at the white house, the actual white house in Washington DC. It's not that her house was beautiful, mine was definitely better than hers; but while I was there, I felt like I was dreaming, I just loved being at her house. I felt different there, that was a weird feeling but that was true. When we got inside of the house, I remember seeing who I later found out that she was Gwen's mother. She really could pass for Linda's sister, little sister even. She was very thin and she had the longest legs ever. She wearing a blue mini dress and some heels; she looked like a stripper. She was also making out with a guy whose mustache was so long that I couldn't decide whether she was kissing the man or the mustache.

"Hey mom", Gwen said as seeing her mom kissing a random guy was usual.

"Oh hey sweetie" her mom answered, I see you have some unusual guests.

Unusual guests, it's obvious that she meant me. I hated Gwen's mom the first time I met her. She looked at me from head to toe as if she had never seen someone so disgusting in her life. She gave me a strange look as she wanted to tell me to get the hell out of her house. I felt very uncomfortable, I wanted to leave. But I pretended I didn't even notice her attitude. I wasn't going to ruin my new life for a drunken lady.

Gwen: This is Victoria; she just transferred to my school.

Victoria: Hi

Gwen's mom: Hello, I'm Linda.

Gwen: Come on upstairs guys.

Gwen: So Victoria, welcome to my room. And my closet. Now take off these clothes, when you're friend with fabulous you got to act and dress like fabulous.

I didn't know what she meant by that. But I do remember how beautiful her closet was. Not as big as mine but a lot more fashionable than mine.

I really had no idea what the girls were up to. I had to stay silent and let them do what they wanted to do with me. Everything went so fast that I don't even remember if they had done my hair first, or my face. All I know is after exactly thirty minutes, when I looked in the mirror, I couldn't even recognize myself. For a while I felt like I looked just like Gwen, even better looking than her. I never thought I would look so beautiful with straight and shiny hair and nice clothes. My huge glasses, my old blue dress were gone, the girls gave me new clothes, new shoes and other words a new look, a makeover.

When I looked at Gwen's closet, I felt like I was looking at stars in the sky. Her clothes were glamorous. Everything was spectacular; her purses, her shoes were all beautiful, I was so jealous of her. I admired her luxurious clothes like I was a poor girl who has never seen expensive clothes before, I wasn't though. When I moved to Los Angeles, I could afford everything she had; I just had no sense of fashion.

"Go ahead and take whatever you want" Gwen said.

"Oh no, I can't' take your clothes".

"Sure you can" that's what friends do Vick. Besides I have way too many clothes."

"Thank you. You guys are so nice to me.

Alicia: You're welcome.

After doing all of this for me, I could just buy the world for Gwen. I loved her with all my heart for doing this to me, I was very grateful to her and I would do just about anything for her to show her my gratitude.

Victoria: I think it's time that I get home, my mom is probably worrying sick about me.

Alicia: I'll give you a ride; um I should be heading home too.

Victoria: Thanks Alicia.

Gwen: See you tomorrow.

Gwen hugged me before I left. I still couldn't believe my new look. As I was leaving, Linda looked at me like she just saw a raccoon transformed into a puppy. She didn't say anything but I could see it from the way she looked at me. Not the same way she looked at me before, but more of a surprised way. I wanted to tell her, see Linda don't judge people by their first appearances, now I'm ten times better looking than you. But I simply said Goodbye Linda. She didn't answer me, her mouth stayed opened for the whole time.

Alicia and Stacey gave me a ride home. It was unbelievable how Stacey had barely talked to me the whole time I knew her. I had a feeling about her, my guts was telling me that Stacey was probably like me once before she started to hang out with Gwen, the poison. It made me feel so good to know that I wasn't the only pathetic one who was hanging out with Gwen. Stacey was just as pretty as Gwen but her attitude was different, she was not just a quiet person, she was a little weird and boring.

Linda: So, first time I see you hanging out with a nerd. What's special about her?

Gwen: Money.

Linda: What?

Gwen: She just moved here from her dad's farm in Kentucky.

Linda: Okay, what's special about her?

Gwen: Mom would you let me finish. She has money, okay, her dad just died leaving her with fifty million dollars.

Linda: Fifty million dollars. Wow, so when are we going to rob her.

Gwen: Rob her are you crazy? We're not going to rob her; we'll make her to give us her money.

Linda: um... that's robbery.

Gwen: (lighting up a cigarette) no it's not. I will be friends with her, I will make her feel special, make her popular, and then she'll do anything for me because she'll feel that she owes me something.

Linda: You sure this plan's going to work? I really need the money Gwen, you know it, I steal owe Bobo and he'll be back sometime this week.

Gwen: I know mom. Where are you going?

Linda: Work.

Gwen: You mean party.

Linda: I like to call it work.

Gwen: When are you coming back?

Linda: Probably tomorrow.

Gwen: or the day after.

Linda: well a women got to do whatever it takes to pay the bills right.

Gwen: Right, drive safe and don't drink too much.

That night, the first time when Stacey and Alicia got to see my house, they looked even more surprised than I was; me being the one who never seen a real house before. They kept staring at it.

"Is this really where you live", Alicia asked.

"Of course" I replied.

"You are different from the other geeks", I mean small town people don't usually live in these mansions when they come to a new city, I must say I'm impressed".

I was waiting for Stacey to say something. I think she saw it in my face too. You know when a dog gives you that look when they need food, that's what I did to Stacey. I stared at her waiting for her to compliment me for my house. I don't even know why I did that.

"Nice crib", she said finally. I still couldn't understand why Alicia was so surprised to see my house. I know my house was a chateau but I didn't expect her who are said to be city girls so surprised of seeing a mansion. It made me realize that maybe these girls were popular because they were hot as hell. None of these girls had what you would say a real house. Stacey lived in an apartment with some foster parents. Alicia spent most of her life at Gwen's house I don't even know if she has a home. And Gwen's house was definitely not nice as mine. This particular fact made me think that maybe these girls wanted to be my friend because I had money. And I didn't mind it at all. I felt like I had power. I didn't show it to them, I showed them that I was inexperience, that I didn't notice anything at all while in my head, I thought I was better than them because I had money. I thought it could buy me everything, including love. I still thought Gwen's friendship was real, they were all really nice to me and they was no way I thought they could be manipulating me.

As Alicia and Stacey left my house, I quickly got inside to explain to my mom my wonderful first day of school. My mom didn't even bother ask me how was my first day. Well who seriously would; my new look definitely tells that I had a nice day and I met great friends. I do remember how astonished my mom looked when she saw me; I think she was happy and surprised at the same time. "Vicky what did you do to yourself"? She asked me." You like it, my friends gave me a makeover mommy" like I remember telling her from my old days when I was playing dress up parties.

"You look beautiful" she said.

"Thanks mom".

"Well, I'm guessing you had a great day of first school with you looking so different".

"You bet, I made a lot of friends. At first I thought they were going to be nasty to me, but they're so nice and they love me.

"Well I'm happy for you honey" she told me with a smile.

The next day at school was different than my first day. Every single eye were one me, I waited all my life for this little attention and I had it this day and because of this I loved Gwen.

The first people I saw were Matt and Tamara again. I didn't want to talk to them but I felt a little obligated to after being so friendly to me on my first day.

"Hey guys" I said. Tamara's mouth stayed opened like she's been stabbed. "Wow, you look different", she said. "You look beautiful, you always did", Matt added. "Thank you, Gwen did it for me", I answered them. Tamara looked so shocked when she heard that. "You and Gwen are like best friends now", she asked "Victoria don't think I'm jealous of you but you really shouldn't hang out with Gwen and her friends". "She's right Victoria, they're not who you think they are" Matt added. I pretended I didn't hear what they just said and walked away. I liked Tamara; she was the nicest girl I've ever met. And Matt was so adorable, I liked him a lot, I always wanted a brother like him, calm and sensitive.

Regardless of what Tamara and Matt told me, I walked to Gwen when I saw her in the hallway. She was accompanied with a bunch of people; girls and guys. They are seemed to be in love with her, they were all following her like a dog or like they were her fans and they were trying to get her autograph. Part of me felt like *wow, I can't' believe I'm hanging out with the most popular girl at school* but part of me envied her. For one second, I got so jealous of her and I began to hate her. I wanted to be the one being followed like a celebrity. But what else could I ask for; I was lucky enough to be her friend.

"Hey Victoria, I was looking for you, come on", Gwen told me. "You look beautiful Victoria." Stacey said. "Of course she does" replied Alicia, Victoria you're no longer a nerd, you're one of us now, and when you're one of us that means you're our sister. " That's right' Gwen said, "you're going to be just like us, see that, everyone from school is following us, we're the hottest chicks at school and we can hook up with any guys we want, tell me a guy that you like and you'll have him just like that".

I believed Gwen when she said she would get me any guy I want. Gwen was like my hero, she was powerful. Her charms, her looks have always given her what she wanted. She has slept with all the hot guys at school, so she sure could hook me up with any of them or all of them. But the only guy I liked was Sam, so I told her I had feelings for Sam. To be completely honest, I did have a little feeling for her so-called boyfriend Chris but I kept that to myself, there was no way I was going to put my friendship with Gwen in jeopardy for a guy, our friendship meant that much to me.

Chris headed toward us; he was actually very stunned to see me. "Victoria, wow, you look like a human" he told me. I was thinking the whole time, I'm hot damn it, admit it, I look like a human. Is that seriously the best you can say? I was a little angry at Chris for saying that.

My anger went away when I saw Sam coming toward me. He was the reason why I took this tight skirt from Gwen the other day. And of course just like everyone else he looked staggered. I thought it was cute. "Victoria I could barely recognize you, you look gorgeous", he said. "Thanks" I told him in a flirty mood.

I felt like everything that had happened to me was thanks to Gwen. My new look, Sam, my new friends, these were all Gwen's work. I was so grateful to her that I gave her one of my most precious gifts. "Gwen, I got you something", I told her. "Really, what is it"? She answered impatiently. And there I was, giving her my most valuable gift ever. "This is for you" I said handing to her my diamond necklace. She took the necklace and admired.

"Oh my God it's beautiful. It looks so expensive, is it real diamond"? She asked.

Victoria: It is, it's from my father.

Gwen: Oh no, you really shouldn't give it to me, I'm sure it means a lot to you.

Victoria: It does, that's why I want to give it to you. You deserve it, after everything you have done for me; you let me have your clothes come on take the necklace.

Gwen took the necklace and hugged me. She seemed happy, it was like one of the nicest things no one has ever done for her and I was surprised by it. She hugged me tightly and said she loved me. That made my happy. But really she had all the reasons to be happy because this wasn't just a regular expensive diamond necklace. It was very symbolic.

It belonged to my father. His mother gave it to him. It meant a lot to my father. It was a symbol to the family. This necklace meant that every single member of the family will only have one child. My father gave me the necklace and I was suppose to give it to my kid when I have one but I gave it to Gwen, that's how much she meant to me.

The bell rang and we all rushed to class. I was glad to have all of my friends in my homeroom, including Sam. While sitting in my chair, I saw Sam taking a direction toward me. I looked the other way to show him I was not paying attention to him. Gwen told me when you like a guy you have to play it cool and I guess that's what I did.

"Hey" he said.

"Hey".

"Listen, I wanted to tell you this a very long time but I never had the opportunity, but do you want to go out sometime.

"Yes, I'd love to".

I didn't hesitate for one second to accept his proposal. The moment I've been waiting for has come. Things were getting better and better. I felt like paying Gwen for everything that had happened to me.

When the bell rang, as I was making my way out, I saw was Tamara and Matt chasing me and yelling my name. "Victoria, I thought you might want to come to the study group tonight" Tamara asked. "I can't", I answered, "I promised Gwen to go shopping with her, and besides poetry is not really my thing, maybe another time". I walked away from them and wondered the whole time what kind of losers would buy tickets to assist poetry contest.

Tamara: What's gotten into her?

Matt: Gwen, that's what's gotten into her.

I walked away from Tamara and Matt the moment I saw Gwen. Maybe I was a little insensitive to just walk away from someone who wasn't doing anything but being nice to you but I had my reasons. I would give anything up to go shopping with Gwen. That was one of the best times I honestly had with Gwen. I felt like was getting fashion lessons from Gwen and her friends, mostly from Gwen of course. She made me throw all my old clothes away and bought me new clothes and new accessories. It's so funny how even though they knew I was rich, they kept buying me stuff. I felt like it was charity.

I was excited to go to Sam's party; I thought it could be my chance to tell Sam my feelings. I wanted to look beautiful in his eyes. I didn't want him to pay attention to Gwen or Alicia. I wanted him all by myself.

I wanted to see Sam, but I also wanted to see his house, I wanted to know what kind of background he came from and I was terribly shocked to know that he was living in an apartment with his unemployed adoptive parents. You want to know what shocked me. Well it wasn't the fact that he didn't live in a mansion like me. He was certainly not as poor as I used to be. What shocked me was how really none of them money had and it made me wonder if they knew something about me, if they really wanted me for who I was. I didn't a doubt in my mind that Gwen didn't like me, I was just a little unsure that's all.

Chris came up to us and hugged Gwen. I always feel nervous around him for some reason; he just wasn't my cup of tea.

"Hey beautiful" he said, kissing Gwen.

Gwen didn't answer him. Funny, Chris really liked Gwen but as we all know, Gwen is not the kind of girl who would stick with a guy forever. I wanted to see Sam, nobody else but Sam so I asked Chris where he was. I wanted to be alone with Sam just as he probably wanted to be alone with Gwen so he took me to Sam.

Sam was even more shocked to see me. He still couldn't believe that old nerd had changed. He kept staring at me then he said "nice dress". I wanted to tell him "nice costume" but he was shirtless and all I did was staring at huge abs. Then he finally asked me what I wanted him to ask me: to go to his room. Gwen told me that was the first thing a guy ask a girl wants he wants to be alone with her or when he wants to have sex. I sure hope it was for the first reason.

According to Gwen, you should never show a guy that you like want him too much or he'll play with your feelings. You have to make him come to you, and that's what I did.

We went up to his room and saw these two random geeks making out on his bed. "Hey get out of here", he said were you even invited"? I laughed. Not only Sam was the hottest and popular guy in school, he was very entertaining and that made me like him even more.

As much as I was happy to be finally alone with Sam, I was very nervous. Being so inexperienced with guys, I didn't know what to say or what to do. He kept staring at me and that made me feel uncomfortable. "Your girlfriend would kill me if she sees us here", I said. I knew Sam didn't have a girlfriend, at least I hoped so, that would break my heart to death to know that my first crush was already taken.

"I don't have a girlfriend" he answered, "I 'm waiting for the right one".

"And who might that be" I asked in a flirty mood.

"Someone who's not going to stab me behind my back, someone real", he said touching me softly "you Victoria".

I couldn't help it when he looked at me in the eyes and said the sweetest things no guys have ever said to me. The next thing I knew, I was on his arms. That was the first time I ever kissed a guy and it meant so much to me. He was such a great kisser. I just couldn't believe what he just said. Life was good; I wouldn't give up anything for this moment. I was making out with the hottest and most popular guy in school; I never thought that could be possible.

Everything was going so well until he tried to get a little more intimate. As he tried to touch my legs and pull up my dress, I knew what would happen next so I had to leave.

"Stop... Umm ... I'm sorry it just... I've got to go", I said.

"Victoria wait", he said, "listen I'm sorry if I made you uncomfortable okay, just please don't leave. Go ahead sit down and have a beer with me.

"I don't drink, I'm not suppose to"

"Here's one thing about hanging out with Gwen, do what you're not supposed to do, come on don't reject me again".

He was right; I mean after refusing to sleep with him how could I possible refuse to at least have a drink with him. I somehow felt a little obligated to. I felt like I grew a lot from that night. That was my first time making out with a guy; my first time drinking and my first time doing everything that I wasn't suppose to do.

Alicia, Chris, Gwen and Stacey were getting wild at the pool party. I have never heard such a loud music in my entire life. My mom would freak out but I was actually surprised to see Linda watching her underage daughter and a bunch of under-age kids drink and get so wild.

Gwen: Have you seen Victoria.

Chris: Nope

Gwen: I'm going to check on her okay.

Gwen walked on me and Sam and I did felt a little uncomfortable even though I felt I proved to her that I can get guys just like her. She pulled me by my hand as if as I was a little girl and she was trying to keep me away from fire.

"*Victoria,* I've been looking for you everywhere. Come down to the party." she said. "So there was definitely some intimacy going on in that room".

"I couldn't help it he's too cute".

"Well I'm happy for you. I think that Sam really likes you"

"Really"

"Of course, he liked you since the first day he laid his eyes on you".

"Maybe after the makeover", I said.

Gwen laughed; I loved making her laugh. I wanted her to love me more and more. I wanted her to feel like I was just like her.

Alicia and Stacey were heading to us. Alicia looked horrible, she could barely stand on her feet and she was puking everywhere. "I am so drunk", Alicia said lighting up a cigarette and handing me one. "Thanks, but I don't smoke", I said.

Gwen: Come on Victoria, it's just a cigarette.

Victoria: I really shouldn't smoke, it's not healthy.

Alicia: You know what not healthy, acting like a total geek is not healthy, it's ugly and stupid just like you, Now take the damn cigarette.

Gwen: (hitting Alicia) don't you talk to her like that, Alicia.

Gwen: Honey you don't have to do it if you don't want to, I don't want you to feel pressured by any of us. And please forgive Alicia, she's obviously drunk. You have something to say Alicia.

Alicia: I'm sorry if offended you, Gwen's right, we love you and we just want the best for you.

Victoria: You don't have to apologize to me, I'm the one who choose apologize to you for not taking your cigarette, I'm sorry.

Stacey: You didn't do anything Victoria.

Alicia was in a very bad mood that night. I felt like she was mad at me for some reason. I couldn't figure out what the reason was but I knew she was hiding something from me.

Suddenly, while still trying to explain myself to Alicia, Sam came up to me and kissed me on my cheeks. "Are you having fun?" he said. Not really Alicia answered". That's when I realized that maybe Alicia was jealous of me dating her ex boyfriend. No matter how much I liked Alicia at that time, I couldn't leave Sam for her.

Because of Alicia's attitude I asked Gwen if I could leave the party earlier. I wasn't going to give up Sam for her nor was I going to lose her as a friend. Sam decided to give me a ride home which made me even happier to leave.

Though I wanted to leave the party because Alicia made me feel uncomfortable but part of me felt a little worried. I didn't want Alicia to hate me. I didn't know what to do that day. I felt like I had to choose between Sam and Alicia and I didn't like that.

While making my way out, I watched Gwen's face. She gave Alicia a strange look and she pushed her as she wanted to tell her it's all your damn fault Victoria left. At least I hoped that's what she was trying to say to her. I left the party without even standing up for myself so I was really hoping Gwen had done her work.

Gwen: What the hell was wrong with you talking to her like that? You know you have to be nice to her; I swear if you ruin my plan I'll kill you.

Alicia: Maybe you're being a little too nice to that bitch, I just saw her flirt with Sam and she knows that I still have feeling for him.

Gwen: Get over it; you broke up with him since ninth grade.

Alicia: Are you actually trying to defend Victoria.

Gwen: of course not, Alicia, Sam has absolutely any feelings for her.

Alicia: How do you know that?

Gwen: Because I told him to get close to Victoria.

Stacey: Why?

Gwen: Because as they get more intimate, not only Victoria will do anything for us, her best friends but she'll do everything for her lover.

The more times I got to spent with Sam, the more I was falling in love with him. I couldn't stop looking at his beautiful eyes. He had the nicest smile ever. I had true feelings for Sam but I couldn't show them to him on that night when he was driving me home from the party. I was intimidated by him. I wanted to tell him my feelings for him, how much he means to me but all we were saying were some random things that have nothing to do with us.

When he pulled in front of my house, he looked surprised just as the other girls.

"Is this really where you live", he asked. "Well yeah, "I answered, why would I be here if I didn't"?

"I had a great time with you".

"So did I.

I thought it was way too soon to tell Sam I loved him, so I simply stepped out of the car in a flirty mood, I think. And that was when he pulled me and kissed me like he never did before.

I could feel the fireworks. I liked the way he tasted, the way he held me. Everything was going well until my mom who I suppose was watching me from the window stepped outside and took me away from my beautiful moment. Sometimes I purely wished she wasn't in my life.

She came outside and said "Victoria, honey it's chilly outside, you really shouldn't be here". I know what she really meant and it had nothing to do with the weather. It was like ninety degrees outside. I tried to avoid her by introducing them. "Hey mom, this is Sam and Sam this is my mom" I beautiful said.

"Nice too meet you; you really are beautiful just like your house", Sam said. "Just like my house Hein" my mom answered. "Don't you mean my daughter?"

Sam was intimidated by my mom. I wanted him to come inside, to show him my house and make him like me more but he left.

I could tell my mom didn't really like Sam. I could see it in her face; the way she looked at Sam told me everything. She gave him a look that she had never gave anyone before. She was a sweet lady and if she didn't like someone, she must have had her reasons. My mom was more like an old fashioned country lady and she didn't like guys with tattoos and piercings. I thought Sam's tattoos looked cute and I didn't care what my mom thought of him,

My mom and I had an argument that night. That was the first night we had fought; and that made me realize that I was becoming like Gwen more and more. I knew she was going to talk to me about the whole situation, so I hurried to my room. And that's when she stopped me. "Where are you going, you know we're going to talk", she said. "Talk about what", I answered pretending I forgot what just happened.

"I don't know where to start", she said. Let me just start by asking who is that guy and why are you so late?

"I told you this morning, I was going to go to a party".

"A party? Honey it's two O' clock in the morning. And where did you get that dress. I don't remember buying it for you".

"Mom, would you stop treating me like a child for God's sake"? I was at a party with my friends okay. First I went shopping and then I went to a party, that's it, no more questions".

"How can you expect me not to be upset? I was worried about you, I tried to call you on your cell and you didn't even answer. And when you came, I saw you kissing some random guy; I didn't raise you like that".

"He's not just some random guy, his name is Sam and he likes me".

"We never used to argue like this. Honey I love you that's why I was worried about you. I'm happy that you have friends and you're having fun but for you own safe I want you to go by my rules".

"I'm going to bed"

"I love you".

I do understand why my mom was so worried. Everything was new. She knew I was growing up but she was still worried about me coming home late and kissing a guy I barely knew.

The next day at school, I ran to Matt and Tamara to brag about my night with Sam. "Guess who kissed me last night"? I said. "Who?", Tamara answered with curiosity. "Sam", I answered.

Matt: Congratulations! I'm happy for you.

Matt walked away from me and gave me a sad face. I knew I was breaking Matt's heart by saying it. I don't even know why I told him between me and Sam. I don't know if it was because I was happy and I couldn't help it or because I was trying to make Matt forget about me. I pretended I had no idea why Matt had walked away and I asked Tamara "Did I say something wrong?"

"Actually you kind of did", she said. "See Matt has the biggest crush on you and you broke his heart".

Matt was the sweetest guy I've ever met, I liked him a lot but more like a brother. I could never picture my life with him. I wanted someone who could make me popular. If I broke his heart, well I was sorry, but I didn't have any feelings for him. I would have made a fool out of myself if I had dated him.

When Matt and Tamara left, I headed to Sam. He carried me to his locker and gave me a rose. "A beautiful rose for the most beautiful girl", he said. As the guy who has been called a player, I thought he was the most romantic guy ever, and I was surprised by it. My dad always told me that when a guy gives a rose to girl, that means the guy has true feelings for the girl.

His rose did mean a lot to me. I thought he was really serious about our relationship and he told me he loved me. I was falling in love with him too.

Gwen walked on us.

"Cut it out you little birdies", she said, we've got things to do today.

"Like what", I answered".

"It's a surprise".

"Alright let's go".

"Now?"

"Yeah."

"We're at school".

"Well, we're cutting school".

I didn't want to cut school that day, I really didn't'. "Don't worry babe, no one will even notice, trust us", Sam told me. I couldn't refuse that. I had to prove to Gwen and Sam that I trust them. I felt that I had to do as they said, that was the thing about hanging out with them.

I tried to hide my face with my jacket so no one would see me cutting school. And that's when Tamara noticed I was cutting school so she came toward me. "Victoria, where are you going", she asked; "Please tell me you're not doing what I'm thinking". "Actually she is", Sam said. He walked me to the car leaving Tamara. Sitting in the car, I saw Gwen heading to Tamara. I saw them talking but I couldn't hear what they were saying.

Gwen: Okay geek let me make this clear to you, Victoria doesn't want you as her friend, and she needs to hang out with people who actually matter.

Tamara: You think you can always get away with everything, isn't that right Gwen, I know exactly what you want from her.

Gwen: And what is it?

Tamara: You don't care about her; you just want something from her.

Gwen: Oh yeah! What is it?

Tamara: Don't play dumb with me Gwen; I'm not going to fall for this time. You know damn well who Victoria is-

Gwen: If I were you I would keep my mouth shut and mind my own business.

Finally Gwen left Tamara and took the driver seat. Their conversation lasted for about two minutes. I know they weren't saying nice things to each other because I could see anger in both their faces. I just hoped they weren't talking about me.

Gwen: Are you guys ready to have fun?

Victoria: Oh yeah.

Gwen turned on the music and picture this I was actually dancing and singing, so not me. Sitting in the car with them, I was scared. I was so happy to be with them, to be just like them. But I knew I was destroying my life in a way. Skipping school is the first things kids do when they want to show their parents that they're not going to college. I knew how my mom would be shocked to hear that her straight A' daughter has gone from hero to zero.

"I have changed big time", I told them. "Old country girl is gone".

Gwen smiled and said "I'm so proud of you". "That's why I'm going to give you a surprise".

A surprise, I thought. As excited as I was, I sure hoped it had nothing to do with drugs or any kind of trouble.

Gwen pulls up and front of a tattoo parlor. I have never even been close to one before and everything was new to me. But the romantic part was when Sam holds my hand and gave me a sign. I trusted him with all my heart. When we got inside, there was a huge man with tattoos all over his body, including his face standing in the front door.

He said "How may I help you today Gwen?" I couldn't believe he knew Gwen's name. It looked like this place was also one of Gwen's get away. I wondered if the man knew that Gwen was only seventeen. I'm sure Gwen had probably slept with him too.

"My friend would like to get a tattoo", Gwen said.

He looked at me up and down then he said "And how old is your little friend".

"Very funny Johnson", Gwen said with an attitude.

The man actually looked a little embarrassed. He kept starring at me the whole time like he wanted to tell me something but he couldn't because of everyone who were there.

"Alright little missy", he said "where would you like to get your tattoo".

I hesitated a little bit. I wanted to get Sam's name on my neck but Sam really wanted me to get one on my belly so I went with his choice. And of course I had to have the one that Gwen, Stacey and Alicia had-a flower on the left breast. Alicia and Stacey were practically quiet the whole time.

"Alright. Now it's going to hurt a little but it'll be worth it in the end".

The man seemed to somehow care for me. I think that made Gwen angry. She got up to her chair and yelled at him "John she is not five, okay just get her the damn tattoo and let us get out of her please". I don't know why Gwen was so mean to Johnson. He seemed like a nice guy. If he weren't nice, he would have kicked Gwen out way long.

Finally, I ended up getting two tattoos and eight body piercing. On my way out the man stopped me and said "You seem like a nice kid, don't mess up your life". If I told you I didn't know what he meant, that I didn't know what I was doing was wrong, then that would be one of the biggest lies of my life. Everyone has a moment in their life when they know they're making a mistake but they just can't get out of it, that's what happened to me.

The night was intense, I was a little scared. My mom didn't like Sam because he had tattoos and piercings. My mom judges people by how they dress and what they have on their bodies. Now what would she think about her own daughter, I was wondering.

I let them know I was worried. I said "My mom's going to freak out". "Well, your mom's going to have to know that you're not a kid anymore".

The tattoo parlor, that wasn't the end of the night. We got to do more crazy stuff. Sam and the other girls decided to go home so now it was just me and Gwen. Gwen was never tired of partying. Two things on earth that Gwen could do without stopping for one second are sex and partying.

"Well, it's just me and you now", she said. Its girl's night and I got another surprise for you.

I was thinking wow back up now; we've been out all day I gotta go home. Another surprise you're kidding me. What is it now?

But of course I didn't say that to her. It's not that I wasn't exited or up for any surprises. Believe it or not, I was thinking about my mom.

My mom was worried sick about me. She went to my school and she talked to Tamara. Tamara, can you believe that.

Lisa: Excuse me, would you happen to know Victoria, you know the new girl from Kentucky?

Tamara: Yeah I do. You must be her mom. I'm Tamara.

Lisa: Nice meeting you Tamara. I'm Lisa and yes I'm her mother. So are you her friend?

Tamara: Well, I guess.

Lisa: Well, I haven't' seen her today and I'm worried about her. Do you happen to know where she might be?

Tamara: Um... I don't know. I'm sure she's fine. I got to go. It was nice meeting you.

I knew Gwen was going to take me to one of these psycho places. And she did. For the first time, I got to the bar. That's when I realized that Gwen was capable of just about anything. That girl had connections.

A part of me was full of trepidation. But in the other hand, I really trusted Gwen and I felt like she could really come up with something and save our asses from getting arrested.

"Don't worry", she said. "I got everything under control; Stacey and Alicia are waiting for us there".

Gwen and I got in the bar. Really it surprised me how Gwen knew everyone in Los Angeles. With her look, she could get anything. She made out with the guy that was standing in the front door just to get in.

"Hey babe", the guy said. "I haven't seen you here for almost a week". "Did you find another hobby?"

They kept on kissing the whole time that Gwen forgot if I was even with her. I felt sorry for Chris.

Suddenly the guy turned to me and said "Who is this beautiful girl"?

"That's Victoria", Gwen said with a funny face. "And Victoria, this is Henry".

One thing I realized is that Gwen kind of envied me in a way. Not that she was jealous of me but she would get a little upset when someone compliments me for anything. I could see it right in her face.

All of a sudden, the oddest thing happened. Henry started talking about me and I didn't like that. "Victoria Whites", he said. "I saw your family in the newspaper, sorry about your dad but I got to say, it's worth it".

"It's worth it huh", I told him letting him know that I'm offended. For a while I kept wondering what had happened to the human race. It seems like everyone thought that money was more important that a loved ones. Well they're wrong, WRONG I'm telling you. Trust me I used to think so too and now I wish I could give up anything to have my father back. Anything, including the cars, the money, the houses. Anything for my family.

Gwen knew that Henry was about to say some sick thing. So she took me by the hand and walked away from him. I was wondering how Henry knew about my money. I had no idea my family was on the newspaper. My mom wanted it to be a secret. If she knew we were so famous, she would have moved back to her little farm. She hated people knowing her business, especially one like that. She was afraid that one of us could get killed or kidnapped.

I let Gwen know how hurt I was about what Henry said. Although I was enjoying my new life but I was still trying to get over my dad's death. My dad was the best father on earth and each time I remembered him, each time someone had said something about him, I would shed big tears. I loved my father, I really did.

What I really wanted to ask Gwen was if she knew I was rich. I mean if she knew about the money I had. Huge mansion, big deal anybody could have that. She pretended she had no idea about my father leaving me fifty million dollars. It sure looked like Henry knew something. At that point, I couldn't hide it anymore like my mom wanted me to; so I told her the whole thing, the truth about me.

One thing Gwen was sure good at was pretending. Pretending she didn't know about my father leaving me money, pretending she cared about my story and pretending she wasn't into my money at all. There was no way you wouldn't believe Gwen's lies. She actually shed plenty of tears for my father that she didn't even know. *Gwen, Gwen, Gwen What a fake!*

Stacey and Alicia were waiting for us at the club. If you're wondering how they got in well the answer is simple; they used Gwen's pass.

Alicia came up to us and said "Where the hell were you guys?" "I've been waiting here for half an hour and I was impatient, drunk and horny. Sometimes Alicia could be a slut too. She reminded me of Gwen.

Stacey was practically quiet the whole time. I will tell you this; Stacy was nothing like Gwen and Alicia. Sometimes I wondered why they hung out with her. She was more boring than I was in Kentucky. She looked at me and then she said "This outfit looks nice on you".

"Thanks", I smiled. I may not have showed it to her, but really, deep down inside there was something special about Stacey that reminded me of myself. And that's why I loved her.

Alicia and I hadn't made up since we had fought the last night at Sam's party. I was standing there waiting for her to apologize and she knew it too. Then she came to me and hugged me. "I'm sorry for the way I treated you last night", she said. I believed her and I was happy. I take it really seriously when someone apologizes.

"Yeah that was adorable", Gwen said. "So let's get this party started".

Alicia and Gwen and I were having the best of our life. Anything a teenager wasn't supposed to be doing, that's what we were doing. Partying like animals, drinking, smoking and stripping on the strips poles. Stacey had fun to I guess. Unlike us she didn't drink or smoke but she did dance with a few guys.

When it was about 3:00 AM, we decided to get home. At least I did. Stacey was already gone about an hour ago. She went home with a guy that she met at the club. A guy around twenty two. We were all so drunk and so tired. Gwen wasn't looking herself at all. I've seen Gwen drunk but not like that. So Alicia decided to drive. Not that she wasn't drunk but not as much as Gwen-she could barely stay on her feet. Henry had to carry her to the car.

Sitting in the car, I was wondering what my mom was doing. How worried she must have been. I took a cigarette. I pretended I wasn't worried at all. All I was saying was *I had a great time, who cares about school anyways?* I did have a great time, but being in a car with two drunken underage girls,

God knew what was coming next. Deep down inside, I knew I was destroying myself more and more and I didn't want to get stop. I guess at some point I did enjoy being a good girl gone bad.

I felt like I was in a sorority and I loved my sisters so much that I would give my life for them. Even drunk, Gwen was smiling at me, saying how proud she was of me for being like her.

I went through my phone and I had one hundred and forty missed called from my mom. *I was thinking damn, is she that worried?* I went through my voicemails. I listened to one of them. My mom was saying "Honey it's me I'm really worried about you, I even went to the police. I came to take you after school to go buy you your birthday gifts but you weren't there. Call me back as soon as you get this message. I love you."

Gwen took my phone. She wouldn't let me listen to the rest of the messages. "Your mom is so overprotective", she said. "How do you even survive in this world"?

Both Alicia and Gwen were confronting me about my mom. They were telling me that I'm not a kid anymore, I'm almost eighteen and my mom has no power over me anymore.

"I'll talk to her about that", I said.

"Please do".

Gwen pulled in front of my house. "So we'll come and get you tomorrow around eight o clock" she said. "Come up with a plan to fool your naïve mother", Alicia added. "I will, I will", I said.

My mom saw everything through the window. Guess my plan of coming through the window and pretend I was just in the shower didn't work. She stood there crying but with a lot of anger unlike her old baby cries.

When I came in, unlike other mothers she didn't yell. She simply asked me how my day was. My mom wasn't the type of person who could yell at you and get crazy. She hated people who yell, you don't have to yell to get your point crossed. Just a simple look would tell everything and you'd wish she had yelled.

She looked at me and she didn't say a word for about two minutes. Then she turned to me and said "where were you", in the most polite way you could ever think.

"I was out with my friend", I said trying to end the conversation. "Listen mom I really don't' want you to start...

"No you listen to me now" she said, still calmly. "I am sick of what you're doing to me. She begins to cry a little. "I was worried sick about you. I haven't seen you for the old day and you come and here like nothing's wrong".

That night all I could hear my mom saying was *Blah Blah Blah and Blah.* I was drunk.

I began to yell at her which was so not me. Unladylike my father would call it. I told her to leave me alone, not to worry about me.

She looked at me and noticed my piercings and tattoos. She put her hand on my head like she was checking if I was alright.

"Lord have mercy" she said. "What happened to you? I didn't raise you like this."

"It's my body and I do whatever the hell I want to do, I'm not a kid mom so stop treating me like one", I yelled more than I ever did in my entire life.

"That's it, you're grounded". "For one week, no phone, no TV and no going out at all until you learn to be home at ten".

"You can't ground me". "You're just jealous that I have friends and you don't".

"Well at least I know what kind of friends I should choose. "Tamara is a nice girl, why don't you hang out with her".

"You don't tell me who I should hang out with, do you understand. I turned my back away from her and for the first time she grabbed me real hard and said "Don't you turn your back when I'm talking to you young lady".

She smelled my breath and she knew that I've been drinking and smoking. I pushed her and went to my room. I turned on the radio very loud. She didn't even bother come to my room and make another scene. She stayed in the living room, walking around like a crazy person.

I couldn't stay home, I was so mad at my mother this night. I called Gwen and she decided to take me to her house.

When we arrived at her house, she stayed there for a while. She let a big sigh out then she got out of the car. She didn't want me to come out. She told me to stay in the car until she told me to get out. She stayed in front of her door, listening to her mother talking. I didn't hear what they were saying but I could see just about everything that was happening inside of the house. I saw Linda talking with a huge man. The man didn't look like someone normal, he was big and I saw him hit Linda a few times. I listened to the whole conversation and I saw everything.

Gwen hid behind her door. The man kept yelling and pushing Linda. I mean he hit Linda pretty bad; I thought he was going to kill her. He kept saying "Where is my damn money, you bitch?" "You're going to give me my damn money or I'll kill you." I don't remember what Linda said to him. Everything was so intense. I had no idea who was that guy or what money was he talking about. I had absolutely no idea. The night was crazy. Linda stayed behind her door pretty much during the whole situation. I wanted to go talk to her. I wanted to ask her what was going on and why she didn't do anything about her mother getting beat up but I didn't. I got really scared so I walked home. Gwen was paying so much attention to what was happening with her mom that she didn't even notice me leaving. What the hell was I thinking leaving my mother's house in the middle of the night?

It was about four o clock when I went to bed. My mom didn't even know I left. I had a dream that night The dream was all about me. I was partying with Gwen and suddenly we decided to drive and we killed a pregnant woman. The woman looked so much like my mother. Then the scary thing happened. The woman came back to avenge me; not Gwen who was driving but me.

The next morning, my mom was knocking at my door. It was such a crazy night, the beginning of my nightmares. It was about 9:00 AM on a Saturday. Usually I would have my pajama on but since I was waiting for Gwen to pick me up, I was well dressed. "Honey, open the door", my mom kept saying. I was still mad at her and I didn't want to talk to her. I let her in anyways though.

"You may come in", I said.

"How was your night?"

"Okay, I guess".

"I'm so sorry, baby".

My mom was the most sensitive person on earth. I don't know if it was because of the fact that she wasn't used to it but she couldn't stay mad at me for long. She totally forgot that I was grounded. She hugged me, kissed me and smiled at me. When she was leaving for work, she made me sit on her lap like I was still five. "Can I bring you something", she said with the prettiest smile. For long I thought I was lucky because I had friends and money but now I realize that I was lucky to have such a wonderful mother and I would give anything for her now.

I looked by my window and I saw a bus standing in front of the house. I figured it was Gwen since she said she would come pick me up at my house. Gwen: Okay, rule number one let's be nice to that bitch and rule number two do not say anything involving her fortune or her father's death.

I opened the door expecting Gwen, Alicia and Stacy but the next thing I knew, the entire school was there with Gwen. I wasn't expecting this at all, but I have to be honest, that was one of the happiest days of my life. I mean who wouldn't be happy. I was once the girl who was living in a poor little farm in Kentucky and now I have the opportunity to show over five hundred people my house.

Everyone got in and they were all stunned by my house. A lot of them didn't know I was wealthy. I admit it-Gwen might have been the hottest girl at school and I envied her a little for that but I wouldn't give up my fortune for her beauty. I was winning Gwen. I wanted to be more popular than Gwen and it started to happen since the day I showed the school my house but I still had love for Gwen.

I had no idea what Gwen was up to. I mean she invited the school to my house but she actually threw a party. She threw a party at my house without even telling me in advance and that wasn't even a surprise party.

That wasn't just a regular party. That was probably the wildest party I went to so far. There were a lot of people, including college guys and people from other high schools. Couples making out in my mom's room, in the pool, just everywhere.

Gwen and Alicia decided to take a swim in the pool. Alicia who I thought would join them just stayed still in the kitchen. She looked at me with a face. Not any kind of face, she actually wanted to tell me something. She stared at one of my father's picture and said "That's your dad huh".

"Yeah", I answered.

"You look so much like him".

"Thanks".

"You know, umm I lost my dad too".

"Really".

"Yeah, I lost my biological parents when I was six months old."

"I'm sorry, that must be really sad to lose both of your parents".

"Well I was just a baby".

I felt really bad for Stacey. I know she was pretending that everything was okay but really it wasn't. Poor Stacey; She never got to know her real parents and she lived in a foster home until she turned seventeen.

I decided to join Gwen and Alicia in the pool. "Hello beautiful", Gwen said. "We were just talking about you".

"What about me", I asked.

"We were just saying how lucky we feel to have you as a friend", Gwen answered.

"I'm the lucky one", I said with a smile.

Gwen, who I suppose bring her own drinks because my mom wasn't a fan of alcohol decided to make a toast in honor of our friendship.

To Victoria, my best friend, my sister, my soul mate.

I was speechless. That was the nicest thing she did for me. She made a toast in front of the whole school and she seemed so real. I believed her and I loved her so much.

She made me promise to her that as best friends, there can be no secrets and we have to do anything for each other. "I would do anything for you", I said.

"You would really do anything for us", she asked.

"Yes I would", I answered.

"You promise".

"I swear".

I swore that I would do anything for her and I meant it. But I didn't think I was going to prove it right away.

"Okay, I'm going to ask you a favor", she said. "It will mean so much to me if you do it".

I had no idea what she was going to ask me to do for her. I thought it could be something like rubbing a bank or maybe one of her illegal things but I wasn't even close.

"I need money", she said. "I need a lot of money".

"What for?"

"My mom is very sick, she has a tumor and she's going to die if she doesn't get a surgery, but we can't afford it".

"How much money do you need"?

"Two million dollars. "

"That's a lot of money for a surgery".

"Well, it's not just the surgery". "My mom has been at the hospital for almost two weeks and she doesn't have any insurance".

"I'm very sorry about your mom, but I just don't know if I can get you two million dollars".

"You told me that your dad left you a lot of money when he died".

"I'm underage; I don't have access to the money, only my mom does".

"Well, there's got to be a way to get the money".

"Gwen, I'm really sorry, my mom will never give me or anyone two million dollar unless I get kidnapped or something".

"That's right! Vicky you're a genius".

"Thanks"?

"Now all we need to do is get everyone and tell them about our plan".

"What plan?"

"You getting kidnapped silly."

"You want me to lie to my mom like that? That's like faking my death".

"Victoria you have too; you promised you'd do anything for me, remember".

"Fine, I'll do it".

"Really?"

"Yes".

"I love you".

"I love you too".

A promise is a promise, my mom always told me. Well it wasn't because of a promise, I felt like I owed Gwen that much. Not just because of what she did for me but I would be the biggest hypocrite if I had let her mom die when I know I could have done something to help her. I would never forgive myself if I had let something like that happen.

Before we began the plan of lying to my mother about being kidnapped, I went to her work just to check on her. I felt like I was about to die or run away from home and this would be my goodbye. The only jobs my mom had in the past were babysitting or taking care of the animals in the farm which gave her nothing but just enough to not starve. My mom always wanted to own a restaurant and that was the third thing she did with the money. One of the waiters or whatever she was took me to my mom's office. I wanted to go tell her not to worry about me whatever she hears from me but I overheard her talking to one of her friends. I didn't know if she was a worker at my mom's restaurant or a friend, but they seemed very close and it surprised me that my mother had a high fashioned friend. The woman was reading a journal then she turned to my mom. "Look at that", she said. "Seventeen year old girl missing for over two weeks. "She hasn't got home since she left and went party with her friends". "Oh I feel bad for her parents".

The second I heard that, I knew my mom was going to say something about me; I mean that was such a coincidence, really.

I heard her say it, she said in a very pale face "That made me think about my daughter, Victoria".

"Why?" the woman asked.

"I don't know, it just that she has tremendously changed. She's always out with her friends at night, she even got a tattoo. I was so worried that something might happen to her while she's out with her friends that I had to ground her for the first time, ever.

"Oh, come on Lisa you didn't have to go that far". Listen I'm going to tell you this as a single mother who raised two teenage girls all by myself, that was the hardest job I've ever had. She's just basically getting older and more mature. Come on you were seventeen too.

"It's not the point, she's going crazy, she's always hiding something, and she even smokes and drinks. And the worst are the people that she hangs out with and that so-called boyfriend of hers. I'm so scared for her, she's everything to me. My soul.

She's everything to me. My soul. When you're about to lie to someone or hurt someone, the last thing you want to hear is that person saying how much she loves you. That will make you stop what you were planning on doing which eventually is sometimes impossible when you're doing it for someone that you cared about too.

After overhearing my mother talk, I went to Gwen's house.
Sam: So here's the deal, I'll get a million and you get a million to pay your mom's debt.

Alicia: What about us?

Stacey: Please don't include me.

Chris: I definitely want my cut or there will be killings. That was the plan.

Gwen: Enough already, you'll all get something okay, but the main thing is to get a million dollar for my mom or she's going to get kill.

I went to Gwen's room and there it was-everyone waiting for me to lie about me getting kidnapped. I was thinking why was everyone so interested in that money, including Sam. I thought it was suppose to be for Gwen's mother.

I pretended I didn't notice how they all wanted the money. I sat down on the bed and said "So what's the plan"? I was expecting Gwen to answer it since it was her idea but everyone was giving me orders like the money was going to be theirs as well as Gwen. Sam was the first one to answer and that surprised me even more. He came up to me and kissed me like he was using his sex appeal to get what he wanted. "Well baby", he said. "It's simple I make a phone call to your mom and we tell her that we need two million dollars and she can't call the police". "Just like they do in movies". I was thinking damn you Sam; you're really good at that.

I couldn't believe how much Sam was interested in that money just as much as Gwen. I looked at him and said "Well it looks like you're interested in the money more than Gwen is, come on now it's for her mom's surgery".

"I know that babe", he answered. "I just care about Gwen's mom that's all."

The plan was well set up. It wasn't just a regular kidnapped that any seventeen year olds could plan, it seemed like it was real. They had broken my mother's door, her windows. They broke some of the pictures of me and my dad, and all I could do was shut up and let it happen. Stupid me.

They had set up a camera connection that made them able to watch my mom. She came in the house and she started crying looking for me everywhere, asking me "Victoria are you okay honey?" How could I be okay? I had to watch my mom suffer but more worst I had to watch everyone laugh at her. Nothing was really funny. I was doing all of them a favor. Two million dollars don't grow on trees.

The phone rang and my mom picked up the phone as fast as she could. I was praying she could ignore the call but who would at a time like this.

"Hello", she answered.

"Hello Lisa", Sam said.

"Who is this?"

"Who am I is not important but what I want is what you're about to find about".

"What do you want?"

"Just shut up and listen. I'll make a deal with you. I'm ready to trade what's most important to you to what's most important to me.

"What are you saying"?

"If you do everything I say then everything will be fine. I'll meet you tomorrow at your house and you get me two million dollars and in exchange I'll give you your daughter. It's as simple as that."

"I want to talk to her". "I want to hear her voice please".

I took the phone and I started to shed tears, it was just so painful.

"Mom", I said. "I love you and I'm fine". "Just do what he told you".

"Where are you are you baby?", she asked.

"You don't need to know where she is", Sam said. "She's safe for now". "Just do what I told you and remember one thing, you bring anybody she's dead, understood"?

"Yes".

After the call, I could barely breathe. I was angry. Not just because I was giving away my fortune but angry because I just chose my friends over my mother. Angry because I just saw a different side of Sam that I wished wasn't real. He was so great at it; he seemed to me like it wasn't his first time fooling people like this.

I couldn't hold it anymore so I left the room without saying a word. Gwen noticed me, chased me. She gently grabbed me by the arm and said "Vicky what's wrong? Aren't' you proud of yourself, you just saved my mom's life."

"I am", I answered.

"Then what's the problem?"

"I just feel a little bad for my mom, that's all. I've never heard her cry like that except when my father died."

"Honey you know we're just pretending. Your mom will be fine. I don't want you to have any regrets okay."

"I don't have any regrets. I'm doing it for you.

"That's right and that's the best thing no one has ever done for me. I will never forget that, thanks to you I won't be an orphan".

Suddenly, Gwen phone rang. I thought it could have been the hospital where her mom was supposed to be. Gwen always had of way of hiding things. It's like she knows she's doing it but at the same time she does it gently so you won't make a big deal out of it. You know what I mean. She picked up the phone, looked at the number then smiled and left.

Gwen: Hello.

Linda: Do you have the money.

Gwen: Yes, I got everything taken care of.

Linda: You're the best.

Gwen: I know.

Linda: So are you going to bring it or what?

Gwen: I won't have it until tomorrow.

Linda: What? I have to have it today.

Gwen: Mom how do you expect me to have two million dollars in one day.

Linda: By robbing a bank.

Gwen: Well I didn't rob a bank. I'm taking the money from Victoria. Now I have to go before she sneaks on me and hear our conversation.

Chris and Alicia were still watching my mother's live tape. I took a look at it myself. She was with the same woman she was talking to when I went by her work earlier on. She was crying the same way a child would cry, a pillow between her legs. "You know I keep blaming myself that maybe if wasn't being too harsh on her, if I had just let her go out with her friends all of these wouldn't happen", she said to the woman.

The woman hugged her and said "Oh honey, it's not your fault, there's nothing you could do about it."

Then my mother looked at one of my pictures and started crying again. She kissed at the photograph and said "I just hope she's okay. I just can't' wait to see her and hug her and tell her how sorry I am."

"Did you call the police", the woman asked her.

"I can't bring anybody with me", my mom answered.

"I don't want you to go by yourself, you don't know what might happen", the woman replied.

"And I don't know what might be happening to Victoria now. I don't know if they're feeding her or God knows if they're raping her or doing something bad to my baby.

It was so sad that even the woman who barely knew me was crying just about as much as my mother, expect more silent. I cried too. It's hard seeing someone you love cry like that for something that is absolutely fake.

Gwen walked in and shut down everything. I guess she noticed how sad I was and thought it'd be better not to watch what my mother was going through. Everyone was quiet for a whole minute then Gwen proposed to watch Friday the 13th. It was all calm for a second, and then out of the blue, someone knocked at the door. They all seemed a little shocked; like they were scared it could have been someone they didn't want there. I was about to get the door since I always do but Gwen ran as fast as she could. I've never seen her do that before, she is usually too busy doing her nails to open the door or even get herself a glass of water

A few seconds after Gwen opened the door, I remember hearing a woman talking to her. Her voice seemed familiar but I wasn't quite sure who it was. Nor I didn't catch everything she was saying to Gwen. I do remember the woman asking Gwen "Do you have it". Gwen was telling the woman to leave. When I Gwen came back, I asked Gwen who the woman was and she said it was some weird kids. And I believed her. The truth is I was depressed. I just wanted to lie down and dream about my mother. I really could care less who the woman was.

Sam got up and said, "Well, I need my beauty sleep, so everybody get out of my room. Except for you my princess."

Everyone left the room. I was actually glad. I wanted to spend some alone time with Sam. I had so much I wanted to tell him.

He gave me a kiss. Really, not just a kiss. He kissed me in a tender way but hungry for it at the same time. I was really feeling him. I took his shirt off and felt his abs. It got so intimate that I was so close to let go. But I didn't let go, I stopped.

I know somehow whether he wanted to or not, Sam was feeling me just about as much I was feeling him; at least at that moment.

I got up and said, "I really don't think we should be doing this."

"Come on," he answered.

"It's not you; it's me I just don't think I'm ready to do this. It's a really big step in a relationship."

"When are you going to be ready?"

"I don't know."

"You want to save yourself for marriage. For God sake when are you going to believe that I love you?"

"I do believe you love me."

"You think I'm just a jerk who's trying to sleep with you. Get over yourself."

"Are you mad at me?"

"No. I'm sorry; I don't know what's gotten into me. I don't want you to feel like I'm pressuring you to do anything against your will. You don't have to do it if you don't want to.

Sam was really into it that night. I've never seen him act that way. I've never seen a guy act that way just for sex. I used to think that people make such a big deal out of sex. Some people like Sam do it as a hobby and some people like my mother, think it's a sin unless you're married of course. Either way I'll be honest; I wasn't' saving myself for marriage. But I didn't want to sleep with him so fast in our relationship.

Gwen and Chris were sleeping in Linda's room. For the whole night, I hadn't had one bit of sleep. First it's my mom, then it's Sam snoring but the worst were Gwen and Chris, God knows what they were doing.

Gwen: What do you think Sam and Victoria are doing now?

Chris: Who cares, I just feel sorry for Victoria. She really thinks that Sam loves her.

Gwen: Poor nerd.

Chris: So about that money, how much will I get?

Gwen: Good night.

Chris: I'm serious, how much will I get?

Gwen: We'll figure it out once we get it.

The next morning, we all woke up and gathered in a truck. We were heading to my house to get the money.

Sam gave a call to my mom to let her know that he was there. My mom brought a bag of money and put it in the truck just like Sam had said. She backed up a little then said, "I got you the money. Now I desire to see my daughter". I got out of the truck and they immediately left.

My mom ran up to me and hugged me in a way she's never done before. She kept kissing me, and asking me if I was okay.

"I'm fine mom," I answered.

"I'm so sorry. It's all my fault. I should have never been so harsh on you."

"It's not your fault mom. None of it."

"I'm so glad you're okay. Let's get in. I made you your favorite dessert."

I took a close look at my mom and she was completely broken. Her face wasn't looking the same anymore. Only one night without seeing me and her face had fade away. Eating the apple pie with my mom, I kept thinking about what Gwen and the other ones were doing at that time.

Sam: Two million bucks, fresh and clean.

Chris: Thanks Victoria.

Gwen: I still have to get my mom a million dollars.

Alicia: I'm going to buy a convertible.

Gwen: And I suppose you'll be paying your tuition Stacey.

Stacey: No. I don't want the money.

Alicia: Then how the hell are you going to pay for the rest of the school year.

My mom had thrown a surprise party for me. The door was written WELCOME BACK SWEETY! They all made it feel like I was gone for college and I came back.

All of a sudden my mom started talking about justice, like I was dead. "He's not going to get away with this like that. "Now honey I need you to help me with this, do you remember his face or where you where? Just tell me anything that'll be helpful to the police?

"You can't call the police," I Shouted.

"Why not?"

"Mom, are you crazy? These guys will kill us if they find out that we called the police.

"Honey, listen I know it's really tough. You've been through so much and I understand. If you don't want to do it now, we can do it later. It's your party, enjoy."

"You can't call the police mom, just forget whatever happens, it's all the past, and we need to move on".

"Honey how can you expect me to just forget what happened. What if they come back again and do something even crazier?"

"They won't."

"Honey you don't know that."

"Yes, I do. Just please don't call the police mom, we'll be fine, I promise".

"But..."

"Mom promise me. Promise me you won't' call the police. Please do it for me."

"Okay, I promise.

I couldn't let my mom call the police. Who knows I probably would end up going to jail too. After all, we were all guilty. We were all in this together. I was waiting for Gwen to call me. I waited impatiently because I didn't want to be the first one to call and ask her about her mom.

Gwen: (opening the door) mom

Linda: Hey, did you get it?

Gwen: A million bucks baby.

Linda: (carrying Gwen and laughing) I don't know what I'd do without you.

Gwen: You damn right, so do you want me to go with you?

Linda: Sure, why not.

I made the first move and call Gwen. She couldn't talk to me for long because she was heading to a guy's house. She wouldn't tell me the guy's name but I figured it wasn't just a regular guy. Usually Gwen is the first one who brings me to a boy's house. I felt like she was hiding something.

Bobo: (looking at his gun and the clock and smiling sarcastically) oh Linda Linda Linda you better not be playing games with me.

Linda: You wait for me here okay.

Gwen: Okay.

Linda: (knocking at Bobo's door.) Here I am.

Bobo: (opening the door) What a pleasure to see you. You got my dough?

Linda: Of course, (handing the money to Bobo) two million dollars just as promised.

Bobo: (kissing Linda) that's my girl.

Linda: You would kill me if I didn't get you that money, wouldn't you?

Bobo: You damn right.

Linda: (hugging Bobo) Well, I hope we can still be friends.

Bobo: (kissing Linda) We can be more than friends.

Linda: (stabbing Bobo) Yeah we can be more than friends.

Bobo: (falling down the floor with blood covering all his mouth) You little bitch.

Linda: (taking the money that she brought Bobo and Bobo's wallet and identity) I've been waiting so long to do this.

Linda: (getting out of the house) good bye.

Linda: (getting inside of her car) what?

Gwen: what happened, why are you back with the money.

Linda: Bobo got what he deserved, now the money is all ours babe.

Gwen: (laughing and hugging her mom) all ours.

We were all at school while suddenly Alicia came up with this beautiful new car.

"Hey guys, check out my new car", she said.

"It's gorgeous", I said. When did you buy it?"

"Yesterday. I wanted to buy this car since I was a freshman, but I could never afford it.

I wish I was smart enough to guess where Alicia got the money from. I mean the money, a new car, new outfits all these made such a perfect sense. I guess maybe I was too stupid to realize it or maybe I was preoccupied by many other things. I asked Gwen how her mom was doing. "She's doing just fine", she said.

"Did she get the surgery?"

"Yes, she sure did."

"Well, I'm glad she's okay. You know, I was thinking maybe we could go to the hospital, I would really like to see her."

"That's so sweet of you. But I don't think it's a good idea, you know she's been through a lot of stress and she really needs to spend some time alone."

Here's another thing about Gwen. Her lies are so strong. There is no way you can change her mind or convince her to do something that she doesn't want to do. And there I was, consuming her lies. I gave her the money and I should have been able to go to the hospital. But the woman said no and there's nothing I could do about it but shut up and let it go. She said no and changes the subject.

"So, Sam told me about what happened last night," she said.

"Is he mad at me?"

"No, of course not, he loves you."

"I don't know what to do, Gwen"

"You should do what your heart tells you Victoria, don't do it if you don't want to," Stacey answered. That was the first time she ever gave me advice me.

"What do you know Stacey", Gwen said." "Listen Victoria, there's nothing fun about being a virgin, nothing, and besides what kind of loser is still a virgin at seventeen."

"So what should I do?"

"Just think about it honey, do you really want to wait till marriage which probably will never happen."

The school bell rang. "Let's get in the car," Gwen said. We all got in the car. As we were making our way out of the school, Tamara gave me a look. Not any kind of look. More like a tender look. She wanted to say something to me but she just couldn't.

We were all in the car, ready to leave. Then Stacey got up and said "Sorry guys, I can't skip school today."

"What?" Gwen asked.

"I really got to stay in school this semester and pass my classes; I'm trying to get into Stanford."

Gwen grabbed Stacey's arm, took her out of the car then said "Can I talk to you privately?"

"Sure," Stacey answered.

"What the hell is getting into you?"

"I just think that now that I can pay my tuition, I should be more focused in my future."

"So you used me to pay your tuition?"

"No."

"Now you listen to me. I didn't have to give you anything. That was my money and my plan and I can still take it back from you. It's all up to you."

"So what do you want me to do, Gwen?"

"The plan is not over; I still need more from Victoria. So I need you to get your ass in that car and do as I say, if you want a future of course.

"Okay, fine."

"Good girl."

Stacey and Gwen talked for a while, then they got in the car and off we went. We stopped at Gwen's house and suddenly Linda appears. I was shocked.

She was not looking like someone who just had a surgery. She wasn't even looking like somebody who just got out of the hospital.

Surprisingly, Gwen was probably as shocked as I was. Maybe more shocked. I could see it in her eyes, the way she was looking at her mom.

"What are you doing here?" she asked.

"Yes, what are you doing here? Weren't you supposed to be at the hospital?" I asked suspiciously.

Linda was completely drunk. It's like she had no idea what a hospital was. Sometimes I wonder what on earth was wrong with Linda. I mean seriously. I do understand the fact that she had Gwen when she was only twelve years old but she could still act like a parent. She just didn't care. She didn't care about Gwen getting drunk, smoking, or skipping school. Now I truly couldn't blame Gwen for being like she was. She sure didn't get that far.

I was still confused about the whole surgery thing with her mother. I had to ask Gwen what really happened because I wasn't buying it anymore. I didn't believe her. There was no way she took the money for her mom's surgery, I thought.

I went up to her and said, "Gwen what's going on, did you take the money for your mom's surgery or not?"

"Of course I did. DO you think I would take two million dollars from you just to go shopping? How crazy would that be?"

"I don't believe your mom had a surgery"

"Well she did. Does she have to look like a skeleton in order for you to believe she was sick?"

"I didn't say that."

"Okay, I'm just going to come right up and tell the truth. Te truth is, I asked you this money for Sam.

"Sam?"

"Yes, Sam. He really needed it.

"For what?"

"Well his mom got arrested and he needed two million dollars to bail his mom out and pay for a lawyer."

"So why didn't he just ask me, I'm his girlfriend after all."

"Because he was scared and embarrassed. Come on now, what guy would want to ask his girlfriend something like that. This is not Sam's type."

"So is his mom okay?"

"Yes, she's fine. I'm really sorry Victoria. I hope you understand and please don't be mad at Sam".

"I understand and I'm not mad at Sam."

"Thank you."

I should have learned my lesson and forget about Gwen and her other friends for good. I mean sure I was upset. I knew she was lying but what could I do. Whatever happened already happened. Whether she really gave the money to Sam, which I doubt or whether she took it for herself, nothing mattered. It's not like she was going to give it back. All I had to do was shut up and try to forget everything.

This whole money situation ended and Linda the diva came down wearing a stunning dress. Linda was the most beautiful mother I've ever seen. Her look, her body, her style, just everything about her would attract even a woman, including her daughter Gwen. She was looking gorgeous for her lucky date. But suddenly the police appeared.

The police came in and everyone was shocked. We just didn't know what was going on and why were they at Linda's house. A cop walked toward Linda and said, "Are you Linda Johnson?"

"Yes, I am," she answered. Without any further words, the next thing we knew is that Linda was getting arrested. Yes, they brought her to the police car and we were so shocked that we couldn't even speak.

Gwen was in tears. I've never seen her cry like that. She followed her mom to the car. She kept on grabbing her and pulling her and fighting the two cops. Linda was screaming and crying. She was begging Gwen not to give up on her. I felt bad but I didn't know what to do. First thing that crossed my mind was why was she getting arrested for. Linda might have been a prostitute but I doubted she was a murderer.

Gwen walked in and there was nothing else I could do but hug her and tell her I'm sorry. I always hated it when people do that to me. When my father died, our relatives and friends would come by and tell me and my mother how sorry they were. I hated it. I hated when they felt nothing but pity for us.

I felt really bad for Gwen. I hated seeing her crying. We were all trying to make Gwen feel good. Alicia was being very kind to her. I let her know that I would always be there for her and to not hesitate to ask me anything she wanted. Surprisingly I meant that.

Stacey was rather distant instead of trying to comfort Gwen like we were all doing. Instead of being nice and supporting, she chose to ask questions like: "So did you mom really kill that guy." To be honest, I was glad that Stacey asked Gwen that. I wanted to talk about it so much but I just couldn't. I mean a friend is suppose to be there for you in these hard times and Stacey helped me a lot by asking Gwen these question.

Surprisingly, Gwen totally ignored Stacey. Damn it, I was thinking. I don't know what was troubling me the most. Was it the fact that Linda went to jail or the fact that she really went to jail for killing that guy and Gwen was just lying to me? All of a sudden a lot of thoughts came to my mind. Gwen didn't even want to talk about the whole situation. Instead, she decided to talk about other stuff. It seemed like she got over her mom's arrest really fast. I purposely asked her if she was going to stay in her apartment. She said there was no way she would go to a foster care at eighteen. I was thinking why would she bring that up if she believed that her mom was innocent. In her mind, her mom was dead for her and that was the beginning of her new life. What a bitch!

After an intense period of drama, I decided to get home. Unexpectedly, my mom was there. It's like leaving the drama and get back again in the drama. And of course like we always ask when we're surprised to see someone, I asked her what was she doing home. Shocked to see me, she answered, "That's what I should be asking you, why weren't you in school?"

She didn't even give me the time to answer her or try to explain. She just went on like a machine. "I just had a call from your school and they said you haven't been in school for a week. What is going with you Victoria? You're failing all of your classes and you're cutting school. This is going to look great on your college application, huh. Where you really cutting school? Damn it Victoria, say something."

There was really nothing I could say to her after that speech. I just wanted her to shut up and go to sleep. I didn't feel good at all, I felt like puking. I lighted up a cigarette and asked her, "What do you want me to say?" I probably shouldn't have done that. And there the machine went again. "What's happening to you? You're acting weird, you're cutting school, you're having a bad attitude and you even dare to smoke."

"I'm almost eighteen," I answered.

"I don't care how old you are, you have no right to smoke in my house," she replied.

"Don't you mean daddy's house?"

I walked away from her then she grabbed me by my arm. "Don't you dare to walk away from me," she said.

"Don't touch me, what do you want from me."

"I want you to stop all this nonsense. I want you to go to school and graduate. I want you to stop hanging out with your bad friends and I want you to keep yourself out of trouble"

"That's not going to happen."

She began to cry then she said, "Why are you doing this to me? You know I only want the best for you."

"No, you don't want the best for me. You want me to become just like you. Lame and old. You're just jealous of me but don't worry mom I'd be upset too if my life was as pathetic as yours.

These words were one of the meanest words I've ever said to my mother. Looking back at it, I feel so bad for saying these to the most valuable person I had in my life. And now I'm still paying the consequences.

I ran to Gwen's house. I wanted to get away from my mom and I wanted to check on Gwen. She said she was about to visit her mom at jail. I asked her if I could go with her but she refused.

Linda: Thanks for coming honey.

Gwen: Of course, so how's life in here.

Linda: Oh it's just like hell. I'm always in a fight; promise me you'll never do anything stupid to end up in jail.

Gwen: I'll try.

Linda: I want you to take care of yourself Gwen, you're a big girl. I want you to use the money wisely. I don't want you to end up just like me honey.

Gwen: Mom, you're talking like you were going to spend all your life in here.

Linda: Forty years is hell of a long time. I'll be seventy-five when I get out of here and you'll be all grown. I won't even get to see my grandchildren.

Gwen: (hugging her mom) Oh mom of course you will, I will visit you as often as I can. I will never give up on you.

Linda: You promise.

Gwen: Of course.

Linda: (hugging Gwen) I love you, take care of yourself baby.

Gwen: Bye mom.

The next day was my birthday; my eighteenth birthday. I was waiting for this day for so long. My mom walked in my room with a huge box and a cake.

"Happy birthday sweetie," she said.

"Thanks. What's in that box?"

"Open it".

I opened the box and I had exactly what I was expecting. The most hideous sweater on the planet. I tried not to let my mom notice I hated it because deep down inside I knew my mom may not have been the most fashionable woman on earth, well neither was I but I knew that was a horribly looking that sweater was, it came from someone special and that's all that matters.

"I got another surprise for you," she said.

"Okay," I answered."

I was thinking please don't be another sweater or the matching pants but instead my mother trusted me enough to give me my first convertible. I remember the look in her face. She was so happy that day, it's like I was getting married. We talked for a long time, about everything. Then she started talking about college. She asked me if I made my mind yet about which college I would go to. I told her I wasn't planning on going to college at all. And of course like every other mothers, she insisted that I go to college. She said that I had to if I wanted a better life. I was thinking how better could life be with all the money I had. I had enough money to buy school. I always thought that people go to school to get a job and make money. Before I had it all, I used to dream of going to Harvard Law School and become the biggest lawyer in the world. But honestly, after having all that money I realize that school was only for the poor. And I was wrong. WRONG!

About an hour after my mother had left, I glanced at the window and I saw Tamara coming over. I opened the door for her before she even knocked. Part of me wanted to talk to her so bad and the other part was scared that Gwen might actually come over and sees us.

She brought me a birthday cake and a present.

"Happy Birthday," she said.

"Thanks", I answered.

"You're welcome".

"I was just about to head to Gwen's house, do you want to come?"

"I think you know the answer."

"Yeah."

"You know I used to be Gwen's best friend once."

"Really? What happened?"

"I was once just like you. I moved here in my freshman year. I didn't know anybody, I didn't have any friends so I started hanging with Gwen, and she made me feel so special, so beautiful. Victoria, I can totally understand why you're hanging out with Gwen. I mean she's so gorgeous and popular but believe me she is no good."

"Why do you say that?"

"Her and her bunch of friends, all they do is use people. Once you're new and you have something that attracts them, they do anything to get it from you. And that includes pretending they love you. But at the same time they make you feel like one of them, they will play you without you even realizing that. They will make you do terrible things. I'm only telling you this because they did the exact same thing to me and even Stacey."

"Stacey? Stacey is one of her best friends why would she want to manipulate her?"

"Stacey was once just like us, she moved here last spring. She was a great kid with a 4.0 grade point average from a prestigious academy. But when she started hanging out with Gwen, that's when she totally lost it. The thing is when you're hanging out with them, you become one of them.

"What's wrong with becoming one of them?"

"Victoria do you seriously don't see anything wrong with becoming one of them. Look what they've already done to you: They transformed you, they made you cut school and you haven't been in school for two weeks. And that's just the beginning. If you don't get yourself out of this mess right now, it'll be too late when you will try too. Trust me. I'm still paying for what I did. I'm going to leave now. Think about everything I said. The choice is yours.

I should have listened to Tamara and say goodbye to Gwen for good. But at that time, I just didn't believe anything she said to me. I thought she made it all up because she was jealous of my friendship with Gwen.

A few minutes after Tamara had call, Gwen called me and asked me to meet her at her house.

Sam: You know, you really don't have to do this, planning a big party for someone we don't even like. I'm sick of you being so nice to her Gwen, and I'm so sick of pretending she's my girl-friend. How long do I have to keep doing this?

Alicia: I thought the plan was to get her money and we did. Why can't we just leave her now, or kill her?

Gwen: Because I still need her. My mom's in jail and she's going to be there for a long time. I don't have anybody to take care of me or to give me anything.

Chris: You have me; we can move together and have a family.

Gwen: You can't take care of me. You can't give me anything. But you don't have to worry about that. I have a plan to get all her money.

Chris: All of it?

Gwen: Yes baby, all of it.

Alicia: Now you're really going insane. How on earth can you get all of her money?

Gwen: Well, she's eighteen now meaning she is old enough to use the money. And I'll just make sure that she put my name on her will. After all won't have anybody else since her mother will be gone.

Chris: I don't understand.

Gwen: Think sometimes, you idiot. Just imagine how rich we can all be if Victoria is gone. But first I'm going to have to get rid of her mother.

Stacey: That was never part of the plan. I'm not in.

Gwen: Oh yes you are. All you need to do is keep your mouth shut and let me do my job.

Stacey: You can't kill them and think you're going to get away with murder. Killing is unacceptable

Sam: As long as there is money involved, I'm in.

Alicia: She's coming, now quiet.

Gwen: Okay you guys, hit the lights. And as soon as she walks in say surprise. Got to make that bitch love us if we want to be in her will.

I walked in and I realized that Gwen had thrown me a surprise party. There were the whole school and other college guys screaming surprise. I was speechless. I had never a surprise party before.

Gwen came in and hugged me. "Happy birthday," she said. I was in tears. That was truly the most amazing day of my life. I mean everything seemed magic. The big crowd, the presents and everyone saying happy birthday to me. I just loved Gwen for doing this for me.

I came here not expecting a party at all especially after the whole jail situation. I knew it was a little challenging for Gwen to throw that party. So I tried to recompense her.

"I got a something for you Gwen," I told her.

"What is it?"

"It just a little gift to show you my appreciation."

"A hundred thousand dollars, how did you get it?"

"Well, I'm eighteen now, I have access to my dad's money and I know you need it. I mean your mom's in jail.

"Does your mom know?"

"No."

"Thank you so much, you're such a great friend."

I sure was a great friend to Gwen. As a matter of fact I was more than a great friend; I was the world to her. Now we're separated by thousands of miles, I'm wondering if she even remembers that I was the nicest and most sincere person to her. I loved her from the bottom of my heart, I truly did. I wasn't just a pathetic girl obsessed with the most popular girl at school, I was her friend and I truly wish she didn't take that for granted. Good friends are hard to find. I'd pay millions to buy a good friend if I could.

During the whole party the only one who was really on my mind was Sam. I haven't gotten the chance to talk to him lately. I didn't understand what was going on between us. I wasn't sure if we were even dating anymore so I went to him and ask him where we were standing. He smiled, then he carried me to Gwen's room.

To be honest there was a point when I really felt like there was no chemistry between Sam and me but when I see him and when he kisses me; I was back on the same old girl crazy in love with him. I loved everything about him. I thought he was a gentleman.

He put me down the bed and then he asked me to close my eyes and put a beautiful diamond necklace around my neck. I was speechless. I never thought Sam would never do that for me. I just kept crying and hugging and kissing him. At that moment, I knew I was completely in love with him. I felt like I really did change him. He kissed me so gently, so passionate but with hunger and I loved it. I was really getting into; nothing, really nothing could make me stop. I took his shirt off, then he took my dress off. A minute after, we both were completely nude. Before we really did it, he did ask me what happened to the girl who wanted to save herself for marriage. "She's dead and gone", I answered.

I'm not going to lie, maybe it was a big mistake that I even met Sam but I can't say I really regret that night. That was one of the biggest nights of my life. That was my first and only time.

After a few hours, we were both completely wasted; Gwen walked in and saw us. She smiled, that let me know she understood what went on.

She wanted me to come and join her at the pool but I couldn't even get up. You know how lazy a female can be after their first time. For the first time Gwen didn't force me into partying with her. She lets me rest. The party went on for God knows how long. There was a lot of action going on. Any wild thing you could think of that includes sex of course, then drugs, people getting drunk. Gwen told me that some neighbors called the police.

I spent the night at Gwen's. My mother was getting used to that so she wasn't really worried. She was crying of course, but not worried. Gwen came to wake me. "So how was your first time?" she asked. "Great", I answered.

Gwen dropped me at my house and when I got in. There we go again, another drama. My mom was holding my journal. I knew that wasn't going to be good because I wrote everything I did in that journal. Everything I didn't want my mother to find out. She read out loud the part where I lied to her about being kidnapped. Since that day, I've never written on a journal again. I mean really why put your secrets on a piece of paper where anybody can just read it.

I didn't know what to say to her. First of all, she was crying and second of all there was no way I couldn't lie more, I was caught. I asked her what was she doing in my room and why would she read my something so private. She ignored the whole question. I mean that's what every teenagers ask their parents when they get caught on something that was found in their room.

She kept crying and then she said "How could you do this to me". I kept asking her the same question: What were you doing in my room and why did you read something so private?

"Are you on drugs?" she asked

"It's none of your business", I answered.

"Oh yes it is, and you're going to tell me what the hell is happening to you".

"Fine you want to know everything fine, I'll tell you since you probably just read it anyways. I'm on drugs, I smoke and I drink. I'm an alcoholic, a slut, a liar, I love to party, I'm not going to college and I want you out of my life."

"I don't recognize you anymore. Maybe moving here was the biggest mistake of my life, but I'm going to fix that. From now on, you will never talk to your friends anymore and you're going to another school."

"I don't think so. I'm eighteen now and I can do whatever I want."

"I don't care how old you are, you're going by my rule until you start acting like an adult. I can't believe you. You lied to me. You set your own mother up, Victoria. You made me believe that you got kidnapped while it was your own plan; you needed the money for your friends. Why did you do this?"

"Because I didn't know how to come up to you and say guess what mom I need two million dollars for my friend who happens to need it very much.

"So you lied to me instead"

"You would have never given it to me if I had asked you like a person. You don't care about anyone but yourself. So get over it because you're just a selfish bitch.

She slapped me. That was the biggest fight I had with my mother. That was the first time my mom has laid her hands on me. I was very shocked. I told her I hated her.

I packed my stuff and went to Gwen's house. I asked her if I could stay with her for a couple of days until I get my mind cleared. I didn't know what was next for me. I didn't want to go back to my mom's house.

A week went by. I was still at Gwen's. My mom left me over a thousand messages. She sounded really worried and I enjoyed it. I was angry at my mother for hitting me and I wanted to worry her so much that she'd be sorry. I shut down my voice because I didn't want to hear her voice. She probably knew I was somewhere at Gwen's house but she didn't know where she lived.

Weeks went by and I still didn't go back home. It was May; school was almost over. We never went to school thought. Life was the same every day. I bought a house and Gwen and Alicia moved in with me. Sam would come and visit sometimes. Stacey was out of the picture. She wanted to take her studies more seriously because she wanted to make it to Stanford. As for us it was the same old thing. Things got wilder and wilder that sometimes I couldn't even recognize myself. I just didn't care about life. I was having fun and I was enjoying my life.

We would spend the whole night partying in the club, get drunk and go to bed at six in the morning. For dinner we'd order pizza or Chinese; that was our daily meal.

We got drunk every night. I mean DRUNK, really DRUNK. We'd each get at least eighty shots every night.

Then one night; the worst night of my entire life. We were all in the car, I was driving. We were all drunk, including me and I hit someone who happens to be my mother. Yes, I hit my mother, I killed her.

Everyone left the car and I was alone with the body holding my mother's dead body. If it was anybody else, maybe I would leave just like the others did, but I had to call an ambulance.

Since that day, life wasn't the same anymore. Because the victim was my mother, I was sentenced for ten years of jail.

Gwen never came to see me. Tamara, Matt and Stacey came to visit me very often. They all graduated from our High School. Tamara would often talk to me about whether she should go to USC or Harvard. "Whichever one of them would work", I always replied. I was happy for her but I envied her as well. I wish I was her. I wish I had to choose between two prestigious universities. But I didn't have that much options. I had to stay in jail, suicide was my alternative. About three months after my arrest, Matt and I finally ended up being in a relationship. He said he was going to wait for me and marry me as soon as I get out of jail. Two years later, Gwen, Sam, Chris and Alicia were arrested for drugs. They were all sentenced for thirty years.

I can't believe how money can cause death. It really can. I would give anything, really anything for my old life in Kentucky. I killed my mother because I was stupid and also because I was rich. I thought money could buy everything. I used money and such a bad way. I tried to be popular by hanging out with the wrong people. Why couldn't I stick with Tamara, she was a true friend. I wish I had believed her when she told me about Gwen and the others. God, I was so stupid. So stupid to not realize that these people only wanted my money. I should have listened to my mom, to Gwen but it was too late when I realized I was being played like a toy. Being popular is nothing but hard work. Hard work to get in and hard work to stay in. Oh God, if only my father hadn't won that stupid lottery.

My mother died without seeing my face for almost two months. I tried to kill myself many times but I thought there was no point since my soul was already dead. In the future, if my mother opens the gate for me, I don't know what would I tell her. There are not enough words to express how sorry I am. I disappointed my father and my mother.

I hate myself. I really do. I was scared of having children because I thought they might do to me the same thing I did to my mother. Well, a month after my arrest, I found out I was pregnant and I was expecting twins, a girl and a boy. Sam never knew anything about him being the father of these kids.

I'll be okay. Yes, I will. I'm not going to disappoint my mother more. I know that she will always watch me through everything I'm doing and I'm going to make her proud. I'm going to do something with my life when I get out of jail. I'm going to start a career, be a good mother. I made a promise to myself that when I get out of jail, first I would marry Matt like I promised and then I would give away all my money. That stupid money that caused me to be lazy and selfish.

When I was in jail I kept thinking how life is just like a season. Like summer that comes and stays for a short period of time, well happiness comes for a short period of time. Everything can change in a matter of seconds. You could think you have it all but you don't. Money doesn't buy anything but material things that have absolutely no value. If I could buy my mom I would, but I know she's in a better place. That's why God took my mother instead of me. I deserved to die, not my mother. She didn't do anything to have her life taken away. She was the sweetest woman you could ever imagine. She loved me to death. I don't know how I would tell my kids this story.

I keep thinking how just one night can totally change everything. Things will never be the same no matter what. My mother's body on the floor will be engraved in my heart forever. And I will never get over her.

Whatever mistake you make could really affect you or someone you love. If I wasn't trying to be popular, I would never have hanged out with mom and if I just listened to my mother, I would have never left and I would have never token her life away. What really hurts me the most is the fact that the last words I said to my mother were *I hate you*.

What I really want to say is to be yourself and never try to be somebody you're not. One of the things that my father taught me is that life is nothing but a game that you got to know how to play to go to the next level. I didn't really understand what he meant at first. But now I see that he meant that in life you make mistakes over and over and that's how you learn what wrong and what's right and that's how you grow. Growing up, being mature has nothing to do with how old you are. You have to make experiences. I will keep on making mistakes, I know it because I'm a human and I still got a lot of growing up to do. Of course there are certain mistakes that you really don't want to make. But once you make them, you just have to learn and move on. Words can't explain how devastated I was about my mom's death. But god knows why it happened like that. I'm going to teach my kids everything my mom taught me and everything I taught myself by my experiences and it's going to be up to them to play the game. I will never blame my mother for what happened. That wasn't her fault. She was a great mom. I'm the one who messed up.

Always listen to someone you love and trust. You may think you know it all, but you don't. Your parents know it all because they lived your age and they know how it's like to be seventeen and how it's like to be in high school and wish you were on top of the world. We all experienced it. What happened to me happens every single day. They may not have lost their mother like I did but everyone wants to be popular. They want people to know them. The feeling of being alone and invisible is hard.

I was only eighteen when I went to jail. I lost a big part of my life but it changed my life forever. That's my story and I hope it can change your life. I truly hope that what happened to me doesn't happen to you.

Now that you've read the book,

think about these questions and answer them within yourself?

- Which character did you feel most emotionally connected to?
  (This doesn't have to be your favorite character, it can be someone
  who's been in about the same situation that you've been.

- Do you believe that you should completely be somebody else just to
  fit in?

- What was the most memorable thing in the book? (It could be a
  particular scene).

- Overall, what did you learn from this book?

Author's favorite quotes

- "A failure is a chance to try harder".

- "The only failure is when you stop trying".

- "In order to succeed, we must believe that we can".

- "Nobody can make you feel inferior without your consents".

- Make no little plans, they have no magic to stir men's blood and will not be realized. Make big plans; aim high in hope and work, remembering that a noble and logical plan never dies, but long after we are gone will be a living thing.

About the Author

Vanessa Daze was born on May 8, 1993. She began writing since she was about nine. She started writing this novel, "Good Girl Gone Bad" around the mid-year in 2008 and finished it in July 2009. Currently, Vanessa Daze is in High School.